Little George and the Christmas Socks

By Joe Malerba

Illustrated by Mark J. Hoffmann

First printing September, 2018

This book is dedicated to my loving wife Barbara and our three amazing children Matthew, Gregory, and Julia. Thank you for all of your support and love each and every day and for allowing me to share this story with the world.

This is a story about hope, love, and humility. Little George embodies all that is pure and innocent and reminds us to look at moments in life through the eyes of a child. To never stop believing in the magic and wonder of the holidays, and to live life with a curious mind, a humble spirit, and a warm heart. For it is in giving that we receive the greatest gift.

Now our story begins in a place,
oh so merry, in a house on the hill of a town called Westbury. Just east of Nantucket, and north of Great Gorge, lived a Mom and a Dad and a sweet Little George.

And Little George knew that even at two,
when Santa had brought him that silver kazoo,
or when he was four and got presents galore
from that jolly old man who had been here before . . .

This Christmas was different, this Christmas was sweet,
for George wanted something to cover his feet.

"If only I could trade in my old building blocks,
for a pair of those fuzzy old green Christmas socks . . ."

Little George thought this through. He planned this all year. He knew that this present would bring him good cheer. For these were not just any old ordinary socks. These belonged to Santa, who kept them in a box. And once every year on this cold Christmas Eve, Santa would wear them (*for those who believe*). . .
as he delivered the toys
up and
down
every
street,
the fuzzy
green
socks he
would
wear on
his feet.

It's said that these socks had magical powers that would keep Santa going for hours and hours. Little George knew the secret; he had seen them before, on the feet of this human never-ending toy store.

They were fuzzy and green, and sparkled with delight, and would carry this man throughout the whole night. Little George said to his parents, *"I want just one thing, not a puppy nor race cars that race in a ring. What I want is special. They're kept in a box, they're worn once a year . . . they're Santa's green socks!"*

Little George's parents looked at their boy with such shock, *"I don't think Santa would part with even one sock." Now Georgie your wish is unreasonably hard! How shall we ask for this gift — in a card?"*

"Dear Santa,
My Georgie's been a good little boy
but he won't even ask you for one single toy . . .
instead this year whilst setting our clocks,
when you come down the chimney
just leave us your socks . . ."

"Do you see Little George, this request is absurd.
We can't even promise and give you our word.
It just will not happen, and may I repeat, those socks
are not coming off dear Santa's feet!"

So Little George pouted as tears filled his eyes.
He was certain those socks would be his big surprise.
He had dreamt of the moment when under the tree,
those socks would be there to fill him with glee.
He would slip them right on and wear them with pride, and tell all his friends . . . he'd have nothing to hide.

"Go on, keep your teddy bears and stackable blocks, I'm wearing Santa's green magical socks . . ."

But alas that dream ended with one final blow. When his mom and dad gave him a confident *"No."*

So Little George sat in his bed Christmas night, knowing what he had wanted would never take flight. The thought seemed so possible, he thought it quite sure, then George let out a yawn and started to snore . . .

And just as sweet Georgie was dreaming away, Santa arrived before night turned to day. His suit and his beard were all black from the coal, and on his left boot he had a small hole. And before the bells rang from the grandfather clock, Santa noticed he had a small hole in his sock. "*Oh my,*" Santa said, "*this just will not do. I'll need something more than one sock and one shoe.*"

He couldn't deliver the rest of the toys, with a hole in his sock, to good girls and good boys. Now aside from his coughing from fireplace soot, poor Santa was nursing a frostbitten foot.

Little George had awoken to a magical sight. One he'd never forget on this very night. There by the tree stood Santa himself. Little George, in comparison, looked like he was his elf.

"*Santa? Santa!*" Little Georgie would squeal,
"Is it really you Santa? Are you here? Are you real?"

Then Santa looked down at this sweet little boy,
and said, "*Yes, it is I, now would you like a toy?*
"There's toy ponies that gallop, a Frisbee or blocks!"
Then, Little George pointed and said, *"I want your socks!"*

Now Santa looked puzzled, bewildered, befuddled. . .
he sat down by Georgie and leaned in and cuddled.
He looked straight in his face as if their eyes would lock, and said, *"Georgie, sweet Georgie you just want my sock? I've only one now, the other is trash.*
The other sock has a hole and has given me a rash.
I've been delivering toys all through the night, and the hole in my sock has struck me with frostbite."

Then Little George smiled, whilst making a twitch.
"I've got it dear Santa, what if you made a switch?"
And he leapt to the dresser where his dad kept a box and way at the bottom was a pair of new socks . . . they were fuzzy and red and would match Santa's suit. So he pulled off his sock and his worn out old boot. Little George beamed with pride as they made the exchange, the old and the new socks they would soon rearrange.

"Oh Little
George,
these are the
perfect fit. Now
are you sure you
want my socks . . .
That's all?
That's it?"
"Yes please!"
said Little George,
and he took
Santa's socks,
and he whisked
them away and put them in the box.

Then Little George turned with a look on his face that was sad, and remorseful, and looked of disgrace.

"Oh Santa, don't hate me or leave me some coal.
You see, I didn't care that your sock had a hole!
Sure your foot was all frozen and your evening quite tragic . . . but I wanted YOUR socks for their powers and magic."

And with that Little George slumped and he cried and he shrugged, but Santa knelt down and within seconds they hugged. *"My dear child, don't cry, for I'm not upset. I'll share with you a story you haven't heard yet. It's true that at Christmas I travel around, from high in the sky and down to the ground. I stop at each house to deliver the toys to good little girls and good little boys. And I never give up; I travel all night; so by morning time, families thrill with delight. And the reason I do this on Christmas each year, is to spread the gift of love and warm Christmas cheer."*

And with that Santa turned and lifted the box that housed those old tattered and torn Christmas socks. *"These socks, Little George, have no powers at all. Sure, they kept me from stopping or taking a fall. They carried me through forests, and deserts of sand. They traveled the world and every foreign land. They kept my feet moving and helped me climb trees, so to jump on the rooftops without bruising my knees."*

"These socks have been treasured for hundreds of years but they aren't worth crying for with large drippy tears.

The power that kept me from ceasing my route, was the love that I felt both inside and out. It's not this red suit that's as red as a fox, and it's not my belt buckle, or my boots or THOSE SOCKS . . .

The magic you thought that would carry my feet was pounding inside of me beat after beat. It was there all along, right there from the start . . . it was beating inside you, your sweet little heart.

'Tis true my dear boy all that sits in this box, are some fuzzy old whimsical green Christmas socks. Now if you don't want them I will understand."

Then Santa pulled Little George up with one hand . . .

"You can have ANY toy that you choose from this sack, and without any question, I'll take the socks back."

But then something wonderful happened that day.
Something right from a hymn or a psalm that you'd pray.
An act of humility, compassion, and love, as though
inspired by wisdom and grace from above.

Little George wanted nothing else from Santa's red sack.
He would not think of giving those old green socks back.

He looked up at Santa and shouted real strong, *"Some may think it crazy, and might say I'm wrong, but I'm keeping these socks 'til the years do grow quite long. These socks are the only gift I'll ever need. If I trade them for toys it would showcase my greed, and I learned something Santa, beyond wisdom and reason. They're not magical socks that push through this season."*

"It's a love that moves through us in this season of giving. That makes moments special and life so worth living."

"So these socks I will treasure once yours and now mine. And whenever I wear them, they will be a sign . . . of the joy and the love that this holiday brings, when the snow falls outside and the Caroler sings."

"These socks may not possess any magical powers that carry you through the air like meteor showers. They may not keep you nimble or focused and quick, and all this time I thought that they did the trick."

"So Santa, dear Santa, I'll cherish these socks. We'll mend that small hole and keep them in a box. And once in a while I'll slip them on my feet and think of these memories so loving and sweet.

"These socks will mean more than my entire toy chest. Because they came from Santa and now I know best."

"I know that what moves you from nightfall 'til dawn, as you scurry about and pounce over my lawn. As you bring all the toys and wonderful gifts, your heartbeat gets stronger and your spirit lifts. What moves was no power of magic at all. It was the look on children's faces, the big and the small."

So Little George placed a kiss on Santa's round nose, and like a spark in the night away Santa goes! He goes and he goes through the bushes and rocks to the next little house wearing George's new socks.

MERRY CHRISTMAS

So the next time YOU see that jolly old man, don't stare at his face or his pudgy old hand. Look down at his feet and there you will find, a new pair of socks from a boy who was kind.

Little George went to bed and his face was still beaming, this was more than a dream that he could ever be dreaming, and when he awoke from the bells of the clocks, right there on his feet were Santa's green Christmas socks.

The End

About the Author

Joe Malerba is a self-published author and a national advertising sales manager in New York City. Born and raised in Brooklyn, New York, he currently resides on Long Island with his wife Barbara and his three children Matthew, Gregory, and Julia. When he's not writing children's books or connecting national advertisers to local consumers by way of television and digital media, Joe enjoys spending time with family and friends, traveling, photography, and being involved in his local parish, learning and living out his Catholic faith.

About the Illustrator

Mark J. Hoffmann is a self taught illustrator and painter. He has illustrated a series of children's books for the American Etiquette Institute featuring "Eddie Cat" and Kenneth Hulick's "The Boy Who Wiggled His Ears". He also designed pins for Hard Rock Cafe and is a Disney Custom Vinylmation artist. Mark lives in Morgan Hill, California with his husband, Rene Spring. He's the proud father to Jaime, Jeffrey and Lindsay and Papa to his three grandchildren, Brianna, Jolene and Mason. You can learn more about him online at www.markhoffmann.com.

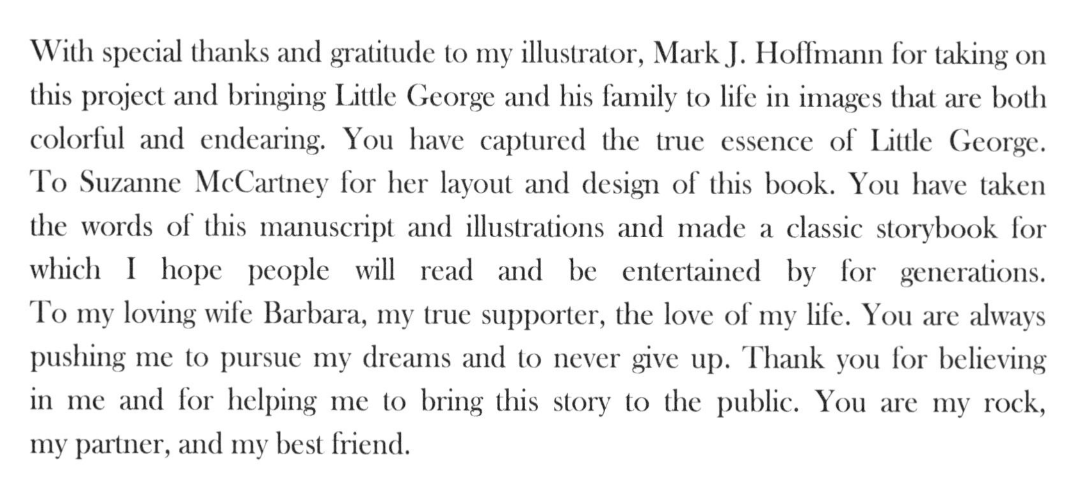

Acknowledgements

With special thanks and gratitude to my illustrator, Mark J. Hoffmann for taking on this project and bringing Little George and his family to life in images that are both colorful and endearing. You have captured the true essence of Little George. To Suzanne McCartney for her layout and design of this book. You have taken the words of this manuscript and illustrations and made a classic storybook for which I hope people will read and be entertained by for generations. To my loving wife Barbara, my true supporter, the love of my life. You are always pushing me to pursue my dreams and to never give up. Thank you for believing in me and for helping me to bring this story to the public. You are my rock, my partner, and my best friend.